1

Izetta

A fictional novella based on true events.

By Tammy Bowers

KDP Publishing, 2017
Exclusively on Amazon
Copy Rights Reserved
https://authortammybowers.blogspot.com

This book has not been professionally edited.
Please excuse the mistakes.

CHAPTER ONE

May, 1944
Oklahoma

"I'm married, Momma." Izetta jiggled the gate open leading to the little yellow house. Smiling so big her cheeks hurt, she grabbed Hunter's hand and jetted up the path. As a married woman, she'd be treated like an adult now. Her three older sisters could no longer call her a child.

"Momma, are you in there? I'm a married woman now." Fingers entwined with his, Izetta took the porch steps two at a time, tugging Hunter along. What would her family think of the amazing news? She couldn't wait to see the look on her sisters' faces. At the screen door, she hollered again and stepped inside. "Momma, where are you? I's married now."

Just then her mother's regal figure appeared in the kitchen doorway. As usual Momma wore a long paisley dress, pink embroidered apron, and black lace-up dress shoes. Wrapped in a tight braid around her head like a crown, Momma's magnificent knee-length hair remained concealed.

Izetta pulled Hunter close and clutched his strong biceps. She couldn't keep from bouncing as she spoke. "Hi, Momma. I'm married. Me and Hunter got married today."

Mother wrung her hands. Her gaze darted back and forth between the newlyweds.

Izetta pinched her husband.

Hunter swiped off his dusty field hat and tilted his face down, as if bowing in prayer. He said nothing.

She focused back on her mother and squealed the obvious. "We eloped."

The lines on her mother's forehead seemed to multiply and deepen, as her eyes narrowed.

"Say something, Momma." Izetta thrust out a hip and raised one fist to perch on her narrow bone. Why wasn't Momma congratulating her on marrying such a fine man?

Oma Belle and Geneva bound into the room, skidding to a halt. Their oldest sister, Otha, was at her own home with her husband and newborn son.

"Look." Izetta extended her left hand and wiggled her ring finger, jostling the thin gold band. She studied her sisters, not wanting to miss a second of their surprise.

Momma shifted, catching Izetta's attention. If possible, the woman's posture grew even more erect. "You cannot get married."

"We already are. I'm here to pack my suitcase. I'm moving to Hunter's house." Izetta couldn't stand still a second longer and let go of Hunter. Both hands lifted to Heaven and she shouted as if in church. "Hallelujah! I'm Mrs. Hunter Avery!" She gazed back at her family. How could they act so reserved in light of the momentous news? Mother tried to teach all of them to be regal, but she and Daddy weren't her boss any more. Neither were her sisters. As a married lady, Izetta could do as she pleased. She did a little dance.

Oma Belle rushed forward and embraced Izetta. "I can't believe it. You're younger than me and married already."

Geneva stepped forward too, but she didn't hug Izetta. Geneva stormed straight at Hunter and slapped him square in the face. "You blasted idiot. She's only fourteen years old."

Hunter jumped back without saying a word, his gaze fixed on the wooden floor.

Izetta shoved Geneva back. "Don't touch my husband!" She wrapped an arm around Hunter and stretched up to kiss his red cheek. When she turned back to her family, she glared at each one while noting their countenance. Oma Belle's jaw hung open, Geneva's chin thrust upward, and Momma—tears flooded her dear sweet mother's eyes.

"Don't cry." Izetta ran forward and embraced the woman she adored. "I'm happy." She led Mother to the rocking chair, helped her sit, then sank to the floor at her feet. Clasping hands, Izetta said, "It is okay, Momma. I love Hunter. He's gotta job, and he's built a room for us above his parent's carport. I can walk over to see you every day. Hunter has it all worked out, you'll see."

"You're just a child. You're only fourteen. You're not old enough to get married."

"How can you say that? You were just fifteen when you married daddy."

"That's why I say it. Fifteen was too young, and you're even younger. You have no idea what it means to be a wife."

"You've taught me to cook and clean." Izetta nodded at her sisters. "I can iron better than any of us girls." She turned back to her mother's lovely face. High prominent cheekbones, thanks to her Indian heritage, and kind brown eyes stared back—so beautiful. Too bad Izetta took after daddy—round face and blonde wavy hair. Izetta shook her head, as if to sling away the thoughts. How could she make her mother understand? Marrying a good man was a dream come true.

"Momma, I know Grand Pappy married you off cause he thought he was dyin'. And Daddy was a lot older than you. Plus, you didn't know him real good, making it hard for you at first. But you grew to love Daddy. What happened to you is different than my experience. I already love Hunter, he's only six years older than me, and we've known each other a long time. See? This ain't nothing like what happened to you."

Izetta nestled her cheek into her mother's palm. Oh how she loved the woman's sweet spirit and laughter. Momma never grew tired of Izetta's stories, daydreams, and reading about faraway places. Izetta could try the rest of her life, and never give back as much love as her mother had bestowed. Without letting go of Momma's hand against her cheek, Izetta searched her mother's eyes. "I love him, and I want to be married. Please be happy for me." She wished she could reach up and wipe away the ugly frowns across her mother's high forehead.

7

Momma sucked in a long deep breath and blew it out slowly. "Promise me you'll finish your schoolin'."

"I promise." Izetta knew how important school was to the woman who could barely read. Mother had to quit school in the third grade to work in the cotton fields. She made sure all of her daughters were excellent readers. Growing up, each sister took turns reading the Bible out loud to the family in the evenings. None of them had trouble sounding out and pronouncing the strange Old Testament names. Nothing seemed more important to Momma than good Bible reading.

Mother bent over and kissed the top of Izetta's head, then moved to stand before Hunter. "I want you to promise me Izetta will finish her schoolin'."

"Yes, ma'am, I promise." Hunter wrung his hat in a circle. His long skinny fingers knocked puffs of dirt onto Momma's clean floor.

After adjusting her home-knitted sweater around her shoulders, Izetta stood and grabbed Oma Belle's hand, giving it a squeeze. Geneva folded her arms across her chest and stretched up to Izetta's height. Even though Izetta was the youngest of four girls, she was the tallest—and the only blonde. Most folks said she was the prettiest, but Izetta only giggled at such nonsense. The dark hair of her sisters resembled their mother's magnificent mane. They far outshone Izetta's blonde curls.

Mother placed a hand on Hunter's shoulder. She curled the other one into a fist and shook it in front of his face. "You ever strike her and my husband will come after you with his shotgun. You understand me, boy?"

"Yes, Mrs. Triplett."

Izetta laughed and rushed to Hunter's side. "Hunter would never hurt me. He loves me." She gazed up at her lanky husband, his sandy brown hair twirled into random ringlets. Despite being slicked back earlier for their secret ceremony, its unruliness won out. Hunter was easily the best looking boy in town, and Izetta couldn't wait for her friends at school to find out they eloped. She'd no longer have to keep their courtship a secret. Izetta giggled at the thought.

The task at hand came back to mind. She led Hunter to the floral davenport. "You sit here and visit with my momma while I pack my suitcase. I want you to call her Momma or Sarah, but not Mrs. Triplett. We're family now." Izetta skipped down the hall, grabbing Oma Belle and Geneva's arms as she passed, tugging them along.

In the small bedroom all three girls had shared, Oma Belle and Geneva flopped onto their double bed adjacent to Izetta's twin. Size wise, Oma Belle resembled their father—short and round, while Geneva and Izetta were tall and thin like Mother. Their oldest sister, Otha, was built in between. All three of her sisters were pretty, especially inside where it counted the most.

Oma Belle elbowed Geneva. "I can't believe you slapped poor Hunter like that. His cheek is still red."

Geneva flipped her hair back. "He's just lucky Daddy's gun's not here." She glanced at her watch. "Though Daddy should be home soon."

Oma Belle might be closest to Izetta in age, but it was Geneva's personality that resembled her's the most—fiery, competitive, and as stubborn as those blasted catfish in Lake Tenkiller.

"You're jealous, Geneva, because I's married and you're not." Izetta yanked the suitcase from the top shelf of the closet and flung it to her bed. While pulling clothes off hangers and folding them into the suitcase, Izetta talked non-stop about how they'd been planning to elope for two whole weeks. "You have no idea how hard it was not to tell you. But Hunter insisted we not tell anyone until he finished the indoor plumbing above his daddy's carport. Hunter said he made it into a proper home for us. There are a few things left for him to do. I haven't seen it yet." She let out a deep exhale. "My very own home, just like Otha."

Izetta stopped her work and clasped her hands above her heart. "Isn't he the most handsome boy you've ever seen? I melt when he looks at me with those copper-penny eyes. He looks so dapper today in his pappy's suit." Pulse racing, Izetta sighed and returned to her packing chore.

Oma Belle got up and dumped the contents of Izetta's drawer onto the bed. All three girls shared one chest of four drawers. Oma Belle and Izetta occupied one each. Geneva had the top two, on account of taking Otha's empty slot when she married Henry and

9

moved out. It appeared Oma Belle was staking claim to Izetta's bottom drawer by placing her own things inside.

Izetta winked at her. "Will you get my toiletries from the bathroom?"

"Sure, Mrs. Avery." Oma Belle giggled as she disappeared through the doorway.

Izetta retrieved her nightgown and stuffed it inside the lacey case with her pillow. "Don't be mad at me, Geneva. Otha got married first, but there's no rule saying we have to get married in order of age. Pete will propose to you soon enough. I'd bet a nickel on it."

"I'm not mad about that, you dim-wit. It's Mother. I've never seen such a look of fright on her before. She's terrified. I don't care if you get married before me. I care that you hurt Momma. She's had it hard and this is a hard time. There's a war going on, but you're always bouncing around here practicing your ridiculous movie-star walk. You need to think about important things. Surely you saw the fear on Momma's face. She turned white like snow."

"I didn't see that, I saw surprise. Besides, she ain't got nothin' to be afraid about. I'm in love." Arms spread wide, Izetta spun a circle. How could she have gotten so lucky?

One look at her sister and Izetta stopped. Nothing she could say would satisfy Geneva. "I promise I'll come over tomorrow and visit Momma. She'll see how grand everything is and that I'm gonna be just fine."

Izetta closed her suitcase and picked it up, along with her stuffed pillow case. "As soon as you tell Hunter you're sorry for slapping him, I'll forgive you and invite you to my very own home for a glass of sweet tea."

Geneva rolled her eyes, and shoved up from the bed. She hugged Izetta tight before whispering in her ear. "I love you, baby girl." Geneva released her and plopped back onto the bed. "But I'm not sorry I slapped your *husband*." Laughter bubbled out of both girls.

Oma Belle returned with Izetta's brush and hair ribbons stuffed into a second lacey pillowcase—Izetta's favorite of her mother's creations. The two girls walked back to the sitting room where Mrs. Triplett and Hunter stared at each other. Palpable silence filled the room. Izetta handed her suitcase to Hunter, and Oma Belle gave him the stuffed pillowcase.

Hunter covered the ground to the front door in three quick steps. "Thank you, ma'am." When he hustled outside, the screen door slapped behind him. "Sorry, ma'am." He called through the metal netting.

Izetta gave her mother and Oma Belle big hugs and told them how much she loved them. "Momma, I'll come by tomorrow to see you and Daddy."

Without another word, Izetta darted out of the house and descended the porch steps. She forced down the lump forming in her throat. How could she be so happy and fight tears at the same time? She refused to look back until she reached the corner. Just before she moved out of sight, Izetta glanced at her family's home. Momma and both sisters stood on the wide front porch under the climbing pink roses. They wrapped all the way around to the side of the pale yellow house. A lone tree stood in the front yard offering plenty of shade and protection. It might be small, but it sure was a pretty sight. At the last second, Izetta reached high above her head and waved goodbye.

Her family waved back.

Izetta kept waving until she turned the corner and lost their view. If only she didn't have to leave.

CHAPTER TWO

Izetta skipped ahead and twirled in a circle as Hunter strolled along, carrying her things. She smiled back at him. "I'm married to you."

He grinned. "Yes, you are."

"What did you and my momma talk about while I packed?"

"She asked if I knew Jesus, and if I would take you to church on Sunday. I promised I would."

"She's always talkin' bout Jesus." Izetta moved to him and entwined her arm in his as they meandered up the dusty road. A few remnants of pink and purple blazed across the darkening Oklahoma sky, sunset long past. "Tell me again about the proper home you built for us." Her insides bubbled at the thought of a room to herself.

"No, I don't want to spoil the surprise. We're almost there."

Hunter had always focused more on work than flapping his jaw. Except when they were alone. But this past week she'd seen little of him. At night, Hunter and his dad worked to install plumbing, so his new bride wouldn't need to go inside her in-law's house to use their privy. During the day he worked at the factory. He'd even seen Momma down there a few times. Hunter said Momma was the best seamstress they had and could sew a parachute faster than anyone else. "I'm sorry, but there's not an icebox yet. I'll buy you one as soon as I save enough money."

They veered in at Hunter's driveway and walked between the house and carport to the backyard. In the darkening twilight, she spied a patchwork flight of stairs up the back of the building. Constructed with new and used boards, Izetta stopped at the base, scanning the chunks of peeled paint all the way up the steep and narrow staircase.

"I built them steps myself. They're safe. You don't need to be ascared." Hunter took them two at a time and set her suitcase at the top. He swung open the rutty door and tossed the stuffed pillowcase inside. "There's no screen on the door yet. I couldn't find a used one, but I did put screens on all the windows."

Hunter disappeared inside with her suitcase. A light turned on before he reappeared on the matchbox landing and motioned her up.

Izetta held onto the rail and tentatively stepped between rotten holes on the first board. More were ferreted through all of the planks. She eased her weight onto the first step. It didn't creak or wiggle, so she pulled her other foot off the ground and peered up at her husband.

A huge grin stretched across his face. "Chicken."

Her confidence in Hunter propelled her up the stairs. At the top, he swooped her into his arms. "I have to carry you over the threshold cause I'm the groom and you're the bride."

Izetta wrapped her arms around Hunter's neck and closed her eyes. He stepped into the room and kicked the door closed behind him. When he set her down, she lifted her lids and gazed around the giant room. Tacked sheets covered the windows. Kitty corner at the far end stood a bed covered by a faded quilt. A matching nightstand and dresser flanked it.

Hunter's chin jutted out. "I painted them sky blue just like your eyes."

"That's real sweet." Izetta ran her hand across the lone rocking chair sitting in the middle of the room. A dingy sheet spread across a small table situated along the opposite wall. Stained drapes cordoned off the back corner. Izetta walked over and peered inside.

"That's the privy. I don't have a real bathtub for you yet. That'll be next."

Opposite the toilet sat a giant circular metal tub that could have served as a watering trough for cows. A ceramic pitcher and bowl scrolled with lavender primroses topped a stand, completing the washroom.

"I know it's not much, but I've only been working on it a couple weeks. I didn't do anything to the walls yet. Thought you might like to wallpaper them."

Izetta nodded. She walked over and hugged Hunter, marveling over his kindness. "I don't care about the metal bathtub. I'm your wife now and this is my home. I love it." She graced him with a big smile, before brushing his lips with a kiss.

When she pulled back to finish her inspection of the room, Hunter wrapped his arms around her and pulled her in. He moved to deepen their kissing.

At the touch of his tongue on her lips, Izetta broke free and ran to the dresser. She slid open each drawer. Only the bottom contained clothes. The rest were empty. "Where's the closet?"

"I haven't built it yet. I ran out of wood."

"That's fine, there's plenty of room in this chest of drawers." She hoisted her suitcase onto the bed. Three drawers all to herself. Plus she was in charge of the house. Izetta couldn't stop grinning. "Tomorrow, I'll take this suitcase back to Momma and Daddy's, and get some pretty things for us. My Momma has sewn lots of curtains, doilies, and quilts. I'm gonna fix this place up real nice."

"Sounds good." Hunter sat down in the chair and rocked while she unpacked.

Izetta had forgotten all about the new walk she'd been practicing for the past two weeks. But with Hunter's gaze following her, she remembered it and slowly swayed her hips as she strolled back and forth from the dresser to the bed. Once the unpacking had been completed, she sashayed across the room and set her suitcase by the door. A quick peek at Hunter confirmed him staring at her every move. The more he watched, the more she swayed.

"It's late." He stood up. "Time to go to bed."

"Okay, I get the bathroom first." Izetta grabbed her nightgown and skipped to the back corner. She stepped behind the curtain and closed it tight behind her. After washing her face and brushing her teeth, Izetta took extra care combing her hair a full one-hundred strokes as her sisters taught her. Once changed, she pulled the drapes back.

Darkness filled the room, but light from the bathroom splashed

14

across Hunter's bare chest. He sat up in bed with the sheet gathered around his narrow waist. She diverted her eyes from his thin white torso, left her clothes in the corner of the bathroom floor, and doused the light. She tiptoed across the darkened room and slipped between the sheets.

"Good night, Hunter. I love you." She kissed his cheek and rolled her back to him.

He laughed. "Funny, Izetta. Come here." He pulled her close and cuddled into her back. He moved her hair aside and planted kisses down her neck.

It tickled. Giggling, Izetta squeezed her eyes shut and scrunched up her shoulders. At the sudden invasion of his hand to her nightgown, her lids shot open. Like the drums on the nearby reservation, Izetta's heart pounded.

"Let's get you out of this nightgown, okay?" He whispered into her ear.

"Why?" Her stomach nose-dived to her toes as uneasiness snaked through her.

"What do you mean, why? So we can make love, of course."

"We're already in love."

Hunter froze for seconds. "Ah…you do know what happens on the wedding night, right?"

Butterflies invaded her belly. "Of course." Although she wasn't exactly sure what he meant, nor was she sure she wanted to know. But her curiosity always won out. "What do you think it means?" Izetta rolled over to see him, but blackness concealed his face. "I can't see you, Hunter. Turn the light on."

He climbed out of bed and hurried across the room.

She hadn't noticed before that the bed stands contained no lamps. Izetta would borrow one of her mother's oil lamps until they could afford to purchase an electric one.

As soon as Hunter flipped on the light, Izetta screamed and covered her eyes. "Why are you naked?" She didn't give him time to respond. "Get your pajamas on!"

"No, Izetta, we're married now."

"So?" She buried her fingers deep into her eyelids and refused to release them. The bed moved when Hunter climbed back in, and Izetta hopped out. Without glancing back, she shot to the bathroom and pulled the curtain tight.

"Izetta, you wanted to be married. I'll teach you what that means."

She didn't know what he meant, nor did she want him to teach her anything. The floor felt like ice on the soles of her bare feet. As fast as her hands could move, she re-dressed.

"Come out, Izetta. It's gonna be okay."

"I'll be out in a minute." She flushed the toilet to cover the sound of her back zipper.

"Izetta, don't be a baby, come out now."

Heat surged into her veins. Why did everyone call her a baby? When she tied her shoes, she yanked the laces so hard, one of them broke. "Drat!" Hunter had ruined everything. She had plans, lots of good plans, but he ruined them all.

After wadding up her nightgown and throwing it to the corner, Izetta yanked the drape back with such force; the tacked ends tore from the wall. The metals tacks spewed across the floor. Her fists formed into tight balls as she marched to the front door, "I'll send my daddy over tomorrow to get my things. Goodbye, Hunter."

She caught a glimpse of his naked body sprinting toward her. "Wait, honey. I love—" He yelped, then hopped on one foot. "Don't go, Izetta."

She slammed the door and raced down the stairs. Not stopping her sprint, she ran to the street, and toward home. At the end of the block, she glanced behind her. No one followed. Izetta slowed to a brisk walk and tromped around the corner. Heart thundering inside her, Izetta seethed. "How dare he!"

Up ahead her parent's house shone in the distance. Daddy's truck sat in the driveway. The full moon illuminated the front yard as if it were a beacon drawing her home. But it didn't quench the fire burning in her belly. Now because of Hunter, she'd have to squeeze back into the stifling room with her sisters, back to being treated like a child—not old enough to date when both of her sisters had boyfriends and Otha had a husband. It wasn't fair. Why did Hunter ruin everything?

At the bottom of the porch steps, Izetta smoothed her hair. She stared up at her house, trying to make sense of Hunter's actions. Once again, fire ignited her insides. Tempted to march back there and slap him across the face, Izetta decided to wait for daylight. Plus, it might be safer to take Geneva with her.

At last she stomped up the porch and yanked open the front door. No attempt to quiet her heavy steps, Izetta stormed down the hall to her parent's bedroom and flung their door open. "Daddy?" Her bellow echoed in the quiet house. "You're gonna have to get rid of that boy for me, because I ain't gonna be a married woman no more."

Izetta didn't wait for his reply and snapped the door shut. She clomped to her shared bedroom and hissed. "I hate boys. I'll never get married again."

CHAPTER THREE

16 years later, April, 1960
Taft, California

"Ah." Izetta inhaled a deep breath of fresh air as the boutique doors eased to a close behind her. Hatbox under one arm, she slid dark sunglasses over her eyes. Their large white frames rested on her high cheekbones. She gazed across the street at a line of palm trees. Southern California seemed so similar, and yet so different from Oklahoma. Their temperatures were nearly identical, but not their terrain. Oklahoma's greenness outshined Taft's by miles. Their deserts were prettier, too. In Taft, green only grew inside the city. The surrounding dessert was so dry, even the cactus struggled to survive. Still, she preferred Taft's starkness over Oklahoma's tornadoes. The mere thought of heading into another underground cellar sent tremors through her.

She shoved the thoughts away and looked to the curb. Now, where'd she park her baby? Four spots up, her '59 Eldorado convertible sat shining under the bright sunlight. A wedding gift from her husband, the flamboyant Cadillac suited Izetta. Even in stilettos and a tight bodice dress, she managed to glide to the trunk of her car and deposit her package.

Izetta retrieved a sheer pink scarf from her handbag, raised it, and let it float onto her hair. The day proved too pretty for the car's top to be up. What use did a convertible serve, if she couldn't be seen driving it? While securing the scarf at the nape of her neck, the squeals of giddy girls drifted through the air.

"It's you! Miss Monroe, can we have your autograph?"

Izetta turned her gaze onto two gushing teenagers. The girls scrunched together and beamed at her.

"Gee, Marilyn Monroe, right here in Taft. I can't believe it." One girl extended a pen and paper. "It's an honor to meet you, Ma'am. May I have your autograph?"

Izetta grinned. "Now what makes you girls think I'm Marilyn Monroe?" To her family and friends, Izetta pretended to detest the common mistake. She had no desire to be a copy of another woman. Only deep inside would she admit how flattering it was to be mixed up for the pin-up star. Izetta didn't think their faces resembled each other at all. But there was no denying how much their hair and figures were alike. Once, while shopping alone in Ventura, she was tempted to play along and sign autographs. But that would never do in Taft. Word of the shenanigan would spread through her hometown as fast as tumbleweed blew across the road leading into the city. And she certainly didn't need any more controversy.

Izetta lowered her sunglasses so the teenyboppers could see her baby blues. "You girls are real sweet, but I'm not Marilyn Monroe. My name's Mrs. Conkey. You may call me Izetta."

Undaunted, both girls turned to each other and clasped hands. They bounced and squealed some more before turning back. "We won't tell anyone you were here, Miss Monroe. We promise."

"Yes, ma'am. Your secret is safe with us." They crossed their hearts.

"Can we please have your autograph?"

"Oh, pleeease!" They gazed at her with big, round eyes.

Behind them a light flashed from the malt-shop doorway. A slim figure slipped out of the shadows, thumbing a silver lighter. He flipped it open, lit the flame and puffed a cigarette to life. He peered over the white stogie at Izetta, and curled his lip.

Izetta froze. Beads of sweat popped up across her forehead, and her palms grew clammy. Yesterday she arrived back from her honeymoon, and so far, she discovered her ex-fiancé following her five or six times. Too many to be a coincidence.

Ford gazed over her from head to toe. His eyes looked almost black, as he licked his lips. Did he think her a slice of peach pie? Pack of smokes rolled into the sleeve of his white T-shirt, he and sauntered her way. "Two weeks." The man mouthed as he slithered closer. Like a gun, he aimed his finger at her. "Boom." Ford's eerie laugh carried across the sidewalk.

Chills torpedoed across Izetta's scalp. Even the California heat couldn't stop goose bumps from covering her skin. "Girls, I'm not Marilyn Monroe. I have to go." She leapt into the front seat of her car, started it with a roar, and screeched onto the street. When she sped through the corner, her right tires thumped up and over the curb. She bounced back onto the street, centered the car in her lane, and floored the accelerator.

Stomach somersaulting, bile rose in her throat. *Keep Calm.* She couldn't risk a fainting spell while driving. Izetta forced in several slow, deep breaths while considering Ford's taunts.

Joe will kill him. Ford had telephoned their house at all hours since returning from their honeymoon. When she first noticed him at the grocery store yesterday, she thought he discovered her there on accident. But he followed her to the library, the soda shop, and even waited outside her mother's house last night. He peered at her through the beauty shop window this morning, and now he had followed her to the hat boutique. All remnants of hope for innocent happenstance slipped away. Why would he stalk her like that?

Izetta struggled to absorb the fact that her ex-fiancé was taunting her. As the richest bachelor in town, he could get any girl he wanted. While engaged, he never acted jealous. Sure, he drank too much and smoked like a factory; otherwise he was smooth and treated her like a queen. Until now.

Her fists squeezed the large steering wheel. Joe would never allow Ford to follow her. Tall and muscular from years of hard physical labor in the desert oil fields, Joe could easily snap Ford's neck. One punch could fracture Ford's jaw and land Joe behind bars. Her breathing quickened. She couldn't let her husband get into trouble for assaulting Ford. Perhaps she shouldn't tell Joe. Maybe she could take care of the problem by herself. After all, she was a modern woman. Independent. Self-sufficient all these years.

Although tempted to flip the car around, she dismissed the idea of confronting her former betrothed on the public street. She left Ford for Joe two months ago, and wished him well. It was high time the millionaire moved on. She had. Why couldn't Ford do the same?

Odd how he accepted her words without anger on the night she broke their engagement. As she had apologized for kissing his best friend, Ford showed little emotion. But now he seemed unable to endure her decision to elope with Joe.

This morning, her beautician shared about Ford getting drunk each night at the White Elephant, spewing threats and predictions. He told anyone who'd listen about giving Joe and Izetta two weeks together, but no more. The man was delusional to think she'd leave Joe after two weeks...or two years, or even two decades. Joe was what she'd been searching for her entire life. She'd never let go.

After eloping at age fourteen, she'd sworn off boys for a decade. She'd been married about three hours and Daddy got the marriage annulled since she had lied about her age. But now at age thirty, she finally fell in love. Real love. True passion. She had no idea marriage could be like that.

Mind settled, Izetta turned at the next light. She would double back and confront Ford herself. Then there would be no chance of Joe losing his temper with Ford.

After rounding the corner, self-doubt crashed through her mind like a tornado. Maybe she should talk to Henry. A well respected and reasonable man, her brother in law could talk to Ford for her. Henry had a gentle way with people. Besides, a lady shouldn't engage in a public argument. Yes. Best let Henry deal with Ford. Otha and Henry talked often about Henry's youngest brother, Max Russell, who just became a California State Trooper. Maybe Max could scare Ford.

Once again her stomach took a nosedive. The police ought not become involved. It could lead to trouble for Joe if he lost his temper with Ford. Idea abandoned, Izetta spun the car around, and drove home. But once in the long driveway of the tiny house they rented from her other sister and brother-in-law, Izetta didn't kill the engine. Foot cemented to the brake, she sat still, clenching the giant steering wheel. How should she handle Ford? Despite being ten years her senior, the man had never been married. He focused on his career and had grown quite wealthy. Shouldn't he be happy Izetta had ended things with him before it became legal? She had saved him from having to pay alimony, His actions made no sense.

"What are you doing sitting out here in the sun? Your shoulders are fixin' to turn pink if you're not mindful."

Izetta jerked at the sound of Oma Belle's voice. Roused, Izetta cut the engine and opened the car door.

"I can't get over this fancy car Joe bought you. Those tailfin things in the back make it look like a rocket ship. Who'd have a mind to build a car like that? You elope with Joe cause he bought you this car, instead of having a proper church weddin' like Momma wanted?"

Izetta squinted down into Oma Belle's wide eyes. Sincerity shown on sister's face—she meant no offense. Izetta chose to swallow the sharp words teetering on her tongue. She pivoted, and paced up the driveway. A full head taller than Oma Belle, Izetta easily gained ground. Her sister raced to catch up while chatting non-stop the entire length of the quaint lot. Their houses were crowded one in front of the other. Loud crunching gravel competed with Oma Belle's babble.

"Merle's taking me to dinner tonight. You and Joe wanna come with us?"

"No thanks, we have plans." Izetta didn't offer any details of her date to the drive-in theater with Joe that evening. She ignored the purple bougainvillea and peach trees she passed, but the sweet fragrance of gardenias bordering her tiny porch stopped her rush to get away. Izetta fingered one of the clean white flowers, with its soft and soothing pedals. She plucked the flower and brought it to her nose. Eyes closed, Izetta inhaled. The gardenia's lovely fragrance seemed to wash away the stench of that nasty business with Ford.

Izetta tucked the flower behind her ear, glided up three steps, and opened the heavy front door. She paused with her hand on the doorknob. In their neighborhood, a locked door wasn't needed. But perhaps she should start locking it until Henry had a chance to speak with Ford and put a stop to his scary antics.

22

Oma Belle clunked up the porch behind her. "Suppose you would have married Ford, if he had of bought you that fancy car instead of Joe?"

Her sister's words cut like glass. No longer able to keep the bubbling anger from erupting, Izetta spun around. "Doesn't anyone get it? I love Joe, not Ford! I don't care if Ford is rich and Joe's an oil worker. It doesn't matter if I've only known him a short time. I'm crazy in love. I wish everyone would just accept it and leave us alone."

Oma Belle's hand shot to her ample chest. Her hazel eyes grew even rounder on her circular face. "Oh, honey, I'm just teasing you. I like Joe better than Ford, we all do. We knew you were only with Ford for his money. We're glad you married Joe instead. He's a good Christian man."

Izetta's eyes narrowed at her sister. "Is that supposed to make me feel better? You thought I agreed to marry Ford for his money? Is that what everyone believes?" She shook her head. "And they call me the dumb blonde. I swear, Oma Belle, God mixed up our hair colors." Izetta slammed the door on her sister's second attempt to apologize.

Once inside her small bungalow, Izetta pressed her back against the door and squeezed her eyes shut. She fought the moisture pooling in them as guilt washed over her. Oma Belle would never hurt her on purpose. She couldn't have known how much Ford put her on edge. Izetta shouldn't take her anger out on her sweet sister. Muffled steps told her Oma Belle had retreated, and for a second, Izetta thought about opening the door to apologize. But she stayed frozen. *Tomorrow.* She'd apologize tomorrow. Tonight, she needed to settle her mind and not let her crazy ex-fiancé ruin her date.

She and Joe had been married exactly one week today. Joe promised to take her to the drive-in theater to celebrate. She wanted to look special for him, and got her hair done and bought a new hat—

Oh drat! Her hat was still in the trunk of the car. Sheer window panel in hand, Izetta moved it to peak outside. No sign of Oma Belle. Perhaps Izetta could make a mad dash to the car and get back without incident.

"Uhh…" An eerie moan broke the silence.

Izetta jerked around, searching the room. From her vantage

point, she could see into the tiny kitchen, sitting room, and stubby hallway. All were empty.

A raspy whisper caused her to leap. "Help." It came from behind her bedroom door at the end of the hall.

"Joe?" She sprinted and yanked open the door. Her gaze froze on the bed as she tried to comprehend the horrific scene before her. Air could not fill her lungs, as she fought to breathe. Knees wobbling, she struggled to take a step, and felt herself collapsing. She sank to the floor. Every ounce of strength she could muster helped her to reach their lofty bed. There she clutched the quilt and pulled herself toward the lifeless form of her husband.

A knife handle protruded from Joe's belly. Blood soaked the front of his plaid shirt and spilled down his side where it pooled on her patchwork quilt. A trickle of blood exited his open mouth. His eyes were closed. The only movement came from a slight flap of his molasses colored hair when the fan passed air back and forth over the bed.

"Joe. Joe. Please, honey. Somebody help!" She screamed at the open window as she clasped his head in her hands. Warm skin passed heat into her fingertips.

Again she tried to suck in air, but her chest had constricted so tight, she couldn't get in enough oxygen to inflate her lungs. Dizziness filled her as the room spun into a black void. Izetta opened her mouth to scream for help, but nothing came out. Darkness consumed her mind as she fell next to her husband's bloody body.

CHAPTER FOUR

Burr...that's cold. Something wet and heavy sat on her forehead. Water trickled down her temple. She reached up to swipe it away, but a hand caught her forearm. Izetta opened her eyes.

"You're okay. I've got you." Joe's smooth voice comforted her like a velvet blanket.

Izetta sucked in a full breath and focused on her husband's face hovering inches away. Deep lines creased his forehead. Perched on the edge of the bed, Joe patted her hand.

It was only a dream—a horrible dream. "Oh, Joe, it was awful."

"I know. It was awful of me. My joke backfired. I had no idea you'd react like that. I'm sorry. It's just ketchup. Please forgive me."

His words skidded across her brain. Her dream had been a joke? Moisture soaked her fingertips, and she lifted her free hand off the bed to find a red stickiness covering it. Izetta bolted upright. A giant crimson pool on the other side of the bed threatened to swallow her bottom. Her eyes narrowed at the large red smear on Joe's shirt. For the first time, the overwhelming smell of ketchup hit her nostrils. Her gaze inched up to Joe's face.

Contorted as if in severe pain, flashes of sorrow seemed to fill his face. "I'm so stupid. That was dumb."

Izetta didn't know if she should comfort him, or scream at him. As usual, her temper won out. "This is your idea of a joke? Let me find you dead with a knife sticking out of your chest? What's wrong with you?"

"My brothers and I are big jokesters. We're always trying to one up each other. Obviously what's funny to a man isn't funny to a woman. I didn't know you'd think it was real. See, there's no blade. I wedged the handle into my buttonhole." He held up a knifeless handle.

Izetta slapped the evil weapon away. It flew across the small bedroom. When the handle struck the floral wallpaper, it left a dollop of ketchup on a marigold before sliding down to the hardwood.

"How could you, Joe? I thought you were dead!" In need of distance, she shoved him away.

Joe made no effort to catch himself and slipped off the edge of the bed. He hit the floor with a thud. "I'm sorry. Can you ever forgive me?"

She'd forgive him soon enough, but wasn't quite ready to say it out loud. Izetta grabbed a yellow shammed pillow, peered over the side of the bed, and swung it down to smack him.

Joe snatched the pillow, stretched out, and tucked it under his head. He winked at her. "I think you're the most beautiful woman in the world—especially when there are flames behind your eyes. You're far prettier than Marilyn."

Izetta rolled her eyes at his ridiculous statement. Her features were much broader than Marilyn's petite nose and mouth. Izetta couldn't come close to the movie star's beauty, but it was sweet of Joe to say.

"You're much smarter and sexier too. Especially when you're fired up. And I know exactly how to fire you up." He reached as if to grab her and tug her down to him.

Scooting away, she giggled and chastised herself for it. Joe could always make her laugh.

"I bought you a new dryer today—a fancy one, worthy of a fancy gal."

"You should have bought a new washer to clean all this ketchup. It better not stain this new quilt my momma sewed for us."

"Oh, baby, the only thing that's stained is my heart with your tears. From now on, it's poems and perfume for you."

She leaned over the side of the bed. "Is that your idea of sweet talk?"

26

"Yes, is it working?" Joe leapt onto the bed, and pulled her into his arms. Lines etched his brow. "I really am sorry. I can't believe I made you faint."

"I don't know why I pass out so easily. My sister Otha does, too."

"Will you forgive me?"

"Of course, I could never stay angry with you, Joe. Just promise you'll never do anything like that again."

"Trust me, I won't." His muscular arms enveloped her before covering her mouth with his. Joe planted kisses along her jaw-line and neck.

All the fire in her belly melted inside his embrace. Since their first meeting, she had no willpower to resist him—though he really must stop buying her gifts. Did Joe think he had to make up for the extravagant life she left behind with Ford? Didn't Joe see how he rescued her? She pulled away and bore her gaze into his. "You must stop buying me expensive presents. The car, my wedding ring, and now a dryer. We can't afford to keep spending money like this."

"Honey, I'm thirty-eight years old. I've never been in love, never been married. Worked my whole life without anyone to spend money on. If I want to spoil you, please indulge me."

She caught a twinkle in his eye, as if he was up to something else. What now?

Joe lifted her hand and kissed the star sapphire wedding ring around her finger. Over a carat and very rare, but that wasn't why she treasured the jewel so much. It came from the man who had captured her heart. Looking back, why had she ever agreed to marry Ford? How had he fooled her into thinking she loved him? Joe came into her life just in time. A light illuminated from Joe like a ray of sunshine exposing the truth—she never loved Ford. Perhaps she had just grown tired of being alone, and loved the excitement swirling around the wealthy oil man.

"Let's get the quilt washed and hop in the shower. I'll clean all the ketchup off you." He flashed a lopsided grin.

Should have known that's what he'd been thinking. Izetta reached out and traced her finger over his jaw and dimples. At his

27

wink, the pounding of her heart increased. Did he have any idea how much power he held over her? Dashing and sincere—how had he remained single for so long? One flash of his sexy smile, and girls would line up to go steady with him. But even with a harem to choose from, his brothers said Joe never paid much attention. No one caught his eye. No one until her. Somehow he'd fallen in love with a small town transplant from Oklahoma. A rare prayer filled her heart. *Thank you, God. I never thought I'd marry after that fiasco as a kid. But now I'm the happiest girl on earth.*

They didn't make it to the drive-in theater that night. He promised to take her the following Saturday for their two week anniversary.

Two weeks. Ford's words echoed into her mind. His prediction that her marriage would fail after just two weeks was ludicrous. Izetta would never leave Joe. Perhaps she should telephone Ford to assure him of her happiness, and ask him to please leave her alone. He was a reasonable business man, after all. She'd not be splitting from Joe ever. Somehow she must put an end to Ford's leers and his gossip around their small town.

CHAPTER FIVE

Top down on the convertible, and a warm breeze blowing the night air, Izetta grinned at her husband as they sat cuddled in the front seat. She raised her Coca-Cola to meet his extended bottle.

"Happy two-week anniversary to my wonderful wife."

It sounded a little corny, but Izetta could only beam at her husband. She clinked her drink against his.

Joe kissed her nose. "I love you."

"Love you more." She steadied the long straw inside her soda pop, and drew a drink. At the sound of the movie, she twisted toward the front windshield. Another pain shot across her shoulder blades. Her muscles screamed at her for all the lifting she'd done the last few days. She stretched her neck from side to side. It felt good to do manual labor, and even better to spend time with her sisters as they packed up Momma's house and moved her across town.

Izetta nestled back against Joe's chest and focused on the drive-in screen outside their car. Warm April nights in Taft were perfect. "This feels so good." Izetta sighed as the music from the speaker lulled her. She closed her eyes and cuddled farther under Joe's arm.

***

The engine roared to life, jolting Izetta upright. "Oh no." She glanced around. "I fell asleep. I'm sorry, Joe. This wasn't much of a date." She scooted along the bench seat to her side of the car. Once again pain throbbed in her back.

"It's all right. You needed to rest. I'll get you home to bed."

Izetta yawned, and tried to stay awake for the short drive across town. Once home, she quickly stripped and peeled off her false lashes. She grabbed a jar of Dorothy Gray Cold Cream to wash away the beauty mark from her cheek. After dousing the bathroom light, she moved to the bedroom and slipped under the sheet next to Joe. "I can't believe how tired and sore I am. All week I've looked forward to seeing *Some Like it Hot* and now I've missed it."

"You worked hard moving your mother. How many boxes of fabric, yarn, thread, and buttons, and lace did you say she had?"

"Over sixty."

"See? And you probably threw your back out lifting that fat wiener dog of hers."

Izetta giggled. "Gretchen doesn't need to be carried. She can waddle."

"Tell you what. I'll take you back to the drive-in next Saturday for our three-week anniversary, and you can watch the movie while I sleep." Again he winked at her.

She loved his wink. He doled it out liberally to her and her alone. Never to another person—not children, not her mother, not even his own mom.

Izetta pulled the little chain on the bedside lamp and darkness filled the room, except for moon beams shining through the open window. She snuggled into Joe's embrace. "Thank you for treating me so special. I don't feel like my skin can hold everything inside I feel for you, Joe. I hope this never ends. Promise me you won't grow tired of me."

"An easy promise to make. I'm the lucky one here. I can't believe you chose me over Ford."

Izetta hugged him tight. "I want you and only you forever and ever." She kissed him goodnight and lifted his arm to ferret closer. She lowered his limb to drape across her body. She and Joe had been married for two weeks now, proving Ford's prediction wrong. She hadn't seen the man in days, but the next time she did, he'd get an Oklahoma tornado of a tongue lashing from her.

She didn't want to think of the man, and shoved the thoughts away. Gaze searching out their window, she took in the night sky. Stars shining bright. Faint sounds of music floated through their half-opened window. Perhaps her nephews were next door playing their records again. Their white lace curtains flapped in the warm breeze. The only other noise came from the standing fan. Joe perched it on the nightstand, so it waved back and forth, circulating warm air across their sheeted bodies. Izetta closed her eyes. The fan's hum serenaded her as she drifted off to sleep.

CHAPTER SIX

"Move, Izetta!"

A sneer jolted her awake. She sat upright, clutching the sheet to her nude torso. Darkness filled the bedroom, but didn't conceal the lone figure standing at the foot of their bed. The air seemed to suck out of her lungs as adrenaline shot into her veins.

Joe yanked his covers back and hopped up.

"Don't move, Joe. I have a gun pointed at your chest. I'll kill you and Zetta if you move. Sit back down."

Familiarity crept into Izetta's brain. *Ford.* Moonlight illuminated him and shined on the silver weapon in his hand.

Joe eased back onto the mattress. "Don't do it, buddy."

"I said I'd give you lovebirds two weeks and your fourteen days are up." Ford snarled at them, his voice deeper than usual.

Izetta scooted closer to Joe. Words clogged in her throat for what seemed like minutes before she finally managed to sputter them out. "Ford, don't…do this…please. You need to—"

"Don't tell me what I need to do. I know what I need to do. Now get out of that bed!"

"Please, Ford, I need my robe—"

Ford screamed at her. "Get out of the way, Izetta!"

Fear propelled her off the side of the bed. She landed with a smack on the hardwood floor. Izetta winced then used her hands to cover her naked body.

A shot from the gun fired, rattling the window. Izetta screamed and scooted into the corner, wedging herself between the dresser and wall. She jumped at a second shot ricocheting through the small house. A puff of smoke filled the room. The distinct odor of gunpowder swirled in the air, choking her as she struggled to take a breath. Dizziness seeped into her brain, as heavy footsteps descended the hall.

Izetta fought the panic welling inside, trying to resist the temptation to run screaming for the front porch. As tears streamed down her cheeks, she swallowed the bile collecting in her throat. She shriveled farther into the plaster at her back, paralyzed except for the quivering of her chin and lips.

The click of her ice box door sounded, followed by its slam and the opening of a beer. Ford's footsteps told her he moved to the living room. She leaned forward slightly, peered around the dresser, and down the stubby hall. Ford plopped into a chair and guzzled.

Izetta's frantic heartbeat launched her forward—she had to get to her husband. Inching down and under the bed, she slithered to the other side. Giant teardrops hit the hardwood as she pushed forward— her mind scrambling to make sense of what had just happened. No longer the man she once knew, Ford had barged into her house and scared them half to death. Surely he didn't really shoot Joe. *No, God. Please no.*

Just as she was about to push herself out from under the bed, a hand flopped in front of her face. She jerked back and coughed down a scream. A glint from the gold wedding band told her the hand belonged to Joe. She reached forward and tugged on him. Limp. Utter limpness. She shuddered, as silent tears poured from her eyes.

"Joe? Please, Joe be okay." She managed to whisper, but there was no response. Then she felt a warm sticky ooze trickle from his hand and onto her fingers. No longer able to bear the sickness rippling through her stomach, Izetta retched. She heaved under the bed, shuddering over and over.

Oh God, please help Joe. With the back of her hand, Izetta wiped the moisture from her lips. She fought the blackness threatening to overtake her mind. Why did she faint so easily? She mustn't let it happen this time. Her husband needed her. Sheet dangling in front of her face, Izetta scooted it aside, and pushed out. Only her head and

33

shoulders emerged. Izetta twisted around and peered at the top of the bed.

Joe's unblinking eyes seemed fixed on a far-away object. Blood drizzled from the corner of his mouth.

"NO!" She screeched and retched again.

A pounding sounded on her front door. Oma Belle and Merle called her name. "Izetta! Is everything all right in there?"

Ford's evil voice echoed through the bungalow. "Stay out."

Icy cold adrenaline shot into her veins. She had to get away from him. Perhaps she could crawl through the window. She forced herself all the way out from under the bed, but froze at the whisper of Ford's voice behind her.

"I can't finish you off, Zetta." His voice lowered. "I want to shoot you, but I can't bring myself to pull the trigger. I planned for the three of us to leave this earth together. I guess only you will survive. I hope you can live with what you've done. It didn't have to happen."

Frozen, she did not speak or move as she stood naked with her back to him. *I need my nightgown—the pink one with white roses Momma made last summer.* She squeezed her eyes shut. What a foolish thought, when her husband lay shot.

The gun blasted, shattering the midnight silence, and a thud hit the floor.

Izetta peered back. Ford's body lay crumpled in an odd position, his face away from her, and the side of his head was clearly visible—what was left of it, anyway.

She raced to the bed and pulled Joe into her arms. "Wake up. We're safe now." He didn't move, his lifeless body heavy in her arms.

Bashing in of the front door sounded, followed by crunching footsteps atop shattered glass. Her sister and brother-in-law called her name. They sounded so far away. Unable to reply amidst the escalating black swirls, she closed her eyes and collapsed.

CHAPTER SEVEN

May 7, 1960 11:45pm

Had it only been a month? Felt like a lifetime—every minute tortured and miserable. Izetta had stayed away from the evil town since the funeral, moving alone to Paso Robles. But with Mother's Day looming tomorrow, she needed to see mom. Close to midnight on Saturday evening, Main Street sat eerily quiet. No wind blew, no tumbleweed rustled, and certainly no love remained for the little oil town in the California desert. Taft, a family-town with Sunday potlucks, church barbecues, and hard-working people, now spread under a veil of murder tainting the wholesome community. As she drove down the main drag, every building looked the same, like nothing tragic had happened. As if her heart had not been ripped from her chest.

Izetta pulled into the parking lot of the White Elephant—the only place open at that hour. In the back row, Merle and Oma Belle's pickup sat alone. She recognized several other cars—the whole gang inside. Could she face their stares? Their questions? Their attempts to offer comfort?

The new wives of ex-boyfriends would no doubt be thrilled to see the dark bags under her eyes and her home-done hair-do. She dreaded going in, but she wanted a drink—several drinks. She wanted to drink enough martinis to sleep through the night in the evil place.

Izetta killed the engine, but couldn't muster the courage to open the car door and leave the safety it offered.

A young couple parked on the other side of her, then strolled arm in arm through the lot and into the bar. Before the doors closed, the distinct voice of Patsy Cline singing *Your Cheatin' Heart,* trickled out from the jukebox inside.

Head leaning back against the blue vinyl, Izetta closed her eyes. She wished for the night when she had passed through those doors and caught her first glimpse of Joe. So handsome. It was the only time in her life that she actually stood and gawked at a man. At the bar laughing, Joe's white teeth gleamed and dimples creased his tanned cheeks. They could be seen all the way across the room. Dark eyebrows and thick lashes framed soft brown eyes. He was the most beautiful man Izetta had ever seen.

He must have felt her eyes roaming over him, because he turned her way. When their gazes met, the smile on his face faded and his mouth opened. His jaw didn't quite drop, but ample space appeared between his lips—his full and perfect lips. He did a periscope dip, looking her up, down, and back up again. Their gazes locked. It seemed to electrify the nerves in her body. New. Disturbing. Sensual.

From across the room, they searched each other's eyes as if they were portals to one another's soul. Her heart rate accelerated as the seconds ticked by. Finally she managed to tear her gaze away, letting it skid across his muscular physique along the way to the opposite side of the room. No sign of her fiancé. Refusing to look back at the man, she continued to comb the room for Ford. At least she tried to locate him, for her mind had stayed glued to the handsome stranger. Who was he?

"Zetta, over here."

Her head jerked back toward the bar. Ford waved his hand over his head. For the first time, she noticed her fiancé sitting next to the hunky visitor. Ford held a frothy beer in his hand and a cig dangled from his lips.

She weaved through the crowd, sashaying her hips slow and sensual, just like she used to practice as a teen, now second nature to her. Most friends and family members had grown used to her movie-star walk. She, too, had grown accustomed to her swagger. But sometimes she noticed the stares of men or the daggers their girlfriends and wives tossed her way.

Ford stood with opened arms. "Hi Zet." She walked into his embrace. When he bent to kiss her, she turned her cheek to his pucker. A cloud of smoke surrounded him. Ford's wet hand from the sweat of his beer stein felt repulsive on her shoulder. She managed an innocent wiggle from his clutch, wishing she hadn't worn her usual haltered sundress. Not entirely true, she knew why she always wore them—Marilyn did. But Izetta would never confess that truth to another soul.

"Honey, I want you to meet a buddy of mine. He's finally returned from an off shore oil rig." Ford scooted a barstool out for her. His breath reeked of beer and smoke.

Izetta eased onto the red vinyl stool and crossed her legs before glancing over her bare shoulder as nonchalantly as she could manage. Spine straight, she tried not to be affected by the dashing man sitting on the other side of Ford. She reminded herself to breathe and not to ogle the stud. Especially not in front of her fiancé.

"Izetta, this is Joe Conkey. He's been a close friend for many years. I've asked him to be the best man at our wedding."

Joe extended his hand and Ford leaned back so Izetta could shake it. "Nice to meet you, ma'am. I've heard plenty about you." His deep voice contained a soothing edge.

When his arm flexed under his short sleeve, she pretended not to notice as she reached for his hand. Gaze inching up to his face, she met a sparkling set of eyes. One winked, and then he graced her with a smile, slightly crooked, and totally sexy. It provided her with a close-up view of his dimples. Her gaze veered to his mouth, where his teeth were as white as his dress shirt. They contrasted with his thick, dark hair—rich like molasses. Izetta licked her lips.

"Don't just sit there like an idiot. Say something." Ford elbowed her.

"Oh. Um, it's nice to meet you, too." She swallowed hard when Joe lifted her hand and kissed the back of it. Try as she might, Izetta couldn't shift her attention away from the handsome stranger. Never in her life had she been so awestruck by a man. Of course she'd been on the defense ever since that immature disaster as a young girl. But here and now, she might drift off to sea with Ford's friend. She flinched, reminding herself that she was an engaged woman. She needed to get out of the water or Joe's current may sweep her away. Izetta pulled her hand back and averted her gaze; afraid he could read her thoughts.

Ford's bark broke the awkward moment. "You two act like long lost lovers. I better not leave you alone." He bellowed, as if his joke was hilarious.

Izetta frowned. *How many beers has Ford had?* The more he drank, the louder he grew.

Joe offered a polite laugh and motioned to the bartender. "Can we get a glass of champagne for the lady? I'd like to toast the happy couple."

A sudden rap on Izetta's car window startled her awake. Silhouetted by the street light, Oma Belle and Merle stood peering inside her car. Izetta didn't want to leave the memory of her first meeting with Joe. Never in all her life had she experienced love at first sight, or even believed it existed. That night proved her wrong. Everything she thought about love changed in less than five minutes.

By the end of the evening, it was clear that she was with the wrong man. Then later that night in bed, she found Joe in her dreams— that night and every night since. A beautiful dream world where of late, she retreated more and more to relive moments with him. If only she could live there permanently, then she wouldn't have to suffer the nightmare of real life.

A second rapid knock on her side window rustled her again to the present. This time she reached down and cranked the handle. "Sorry, I'm not in my right mind."

"It's okay, honey. We understand." Oma Belle reached in and patted Izetta's shoulder. Deep creases lined her sister's face. Even in the dark, Oma Belle's color appeared drained.

Merle pulled a handkerchief from his pocket and handed it to Izetta.

Only then did she become aware of the wetness on her cheeks. She had never been a crier before, but now her eyes leaked like a dark, seeping cave. She took the handkerchief and dabbed her face. "I must look a fright." Izetta extended it back, but Merle shook his head.

"Keep it."

"Thank you." She folded the hanky on her lap, anything to keep her fingers busy.

Merle's deep voice broke the silence. "You're gonna be okay, Izetta. You just need some time. It'll be hard, but you'll get through this. You will be happy again one day. I promise."

She nodded, unable to speak. No use arguing even if she could utter words. She'd never recover from this. Not ever. She faced her sister and brother-in-law, and whispered. "I shouldn't have come back." Her voice cracked. "I can't stay. I...I have to get out of this town."

"It's so late, honey. Why don't you scoot over and let me drive you back to our place. You should get some sleep." Oma Belle reached for the car door.

"No!" Izetta slapped Oma Belle's hand away.

Her sister jerked back and shot a glance at Merle.

Izetta melted. "I'm sorry. I didn't mean to do that. I love you guys. Thank you for the offer, but I can't go anywhere near my old house."

"Oh, of course not. Forgive me for even suggesting it. How about I drive you over to Otha and Henry's? Or to Mother's house— she'd love that." Oma Belle's eyebrows rose high, as if in hope.

The look on her sister's face tugged on Izetta's heart, but she managed to shake her head no. A twinge of guilt rocketed through her and she glanced away. "I can't. I have to go home." Tears flowed again. Home had always been in Taft with her family, friends, and beloved husband. All were lost to her now. The studio apartment near the beach would never be home. When she reached up and smoothed her hair; her trembling fingertips brushed her ear lobes. *Bare.* She hadn't forgotten to put on earrings since she was a teen.

"I'm sorry. Thank you both for trying to help me." Handing over the pink envelope setting on the passenger seat, Izetta said, "Give this card to Momma for me. Tell her I love her and I'm sorry. I really did try. Next year I'll have her over to my place at the beach for the entire Mother's Day weekend." Izetta tried to smile.

Oma Belle squeezed through the open window and embraced

her. Trembling, she began to weep.

Izetta hugged her sister and patted Oma Belle's shoulder. "I love you."

Merle pulled Oma Belle out and wrapped an arm around her. He scooted his glasses up on his big nose and nodded at Izetta. "We'll tell her. You drive careful."

"Goodbye." She started her car and eased onto the street. Reflected in her rearview mirror stood Merle and Oma Belle in a tight embrace. Oma Belle's whole body shook as Merle gave an affectionate rub up and down her spine.

An ice pick tore into Izetta's heart. If only Joe were here to comfort her.

CHAPTER EIGHT

Unable to hold it in any longer, Izetta burst out crying. In the privacy of car, she sobbed as she drove out of town. Her Eldorado seemed to be the only thing moving through Taft, as if it had turned into a ghost town. She accelerated past the haunted memories.

Even when the city lights were barely discernible in her rear view mirror, Izetta couldn't stop the tears stinging her cheeks. Lost to her forever, Joe would never come back. How could she survive without him? After tasting love, a once in a lifetime love, how could she live without it? Clutched in a tight wad, she didn't bother using Merle's handkerchief to dry her eyes. They'd just be wet again in seconds.

Minutes passed before she steadied her breathing. She tried to focus on the road ahead, but her mind jumped from one thought of Joe to another. What would he be doing in Heaven? Could he see her? She finally raised the hanky and wiped her nose.

A picture of Joe's smile filled her mind, as did the memory of their first kiss. The corners of her lips lifted. Their first kiss was her favorite memory of all. Before her, Joe's face came alive and he winked at her. Heat rushed to her cheeks. Izetta reached up and fluffed her bangs. As she zoomed down the road, she could almost hear his words, his warm baritone voice, as if he sat next to her in the car.

Hi, baby.

The memory took hold, crowding out the task of driving across the mountains. She pictured the flex of Joe's arm as he held open her front door on that first night. He had motioned her inside. *I delivered you home and completed my duty as best man.*

"Come in and let me give you a cup of coffee before you drive back to Bakersfield. It's late. You must be exhausted." Was it wise to invite such a dangerous man inside? Not dangerous as in causing harm to her, but dangerous because she might not act like a proper lady. The undeniable pull to this man baffled her. Foreign and backwards. All her life she'd been the one on defense from the opposite sex. Never before had she felt ready to grab a man and kiss him. Yet, her fingers itched to touch his skin. She couldn't look away from Joe's eyes. They were like magnets pulling her in.

Joe stepped into her darkened house.

Izetta brushed his arm as she passed to shut the door. Once closed, she faced him. Unable to step away, she stared into his eyes.

He held her gaze a long moment before breaking away.

Izetta reached out and clutched his arm. "Don't go." She froze at her own words. Where had they come from? She looked down the length of his forearm—strong and bronzed by the sun. She slid her fingertips down to his wrist and flipped his palm up. Masculine. Rough. She ran a manicured nail around each big callus at the base of his fingers.

During her invasion of his hand, Joe remained still and silent, his head hovering inches above hers. His breath on her cheek.

At last he reached out and caressed the side of her face, tracing her jaw-line with his thumb before moving to her hair. A lock lifted and twirled in his fingertips. It dropped and his hand moved to one of her earlobes. He pulled off her clip earring and let it drop to the floor. It bounced on the hardwood, chasing away the silence.

Joe slid his other hand from hers, removed her other earring, and caressed both of her earlobes. His thumbs moved back across her jaw to her mouth and roamed over her lower lip, then up to her eyebrows and down the slope of her nose. He did not kiss her or say a single word as he devoured every inch of her face with his touch.

Stomach somersaulting, she closed her eyes to soak in his touch. No man had ever caressed her face like that before. Tendrils squeezed around her heart. The power this stranger had over her was scandalous.

His hand dropped to her neck and traced the length of her collarbone. When he squeezed her bare shoulder, both eyes shot open and a shiver raced across her scalp.

Legs unsteady, Izetta stepped back and leaned against the wall. The thought to push him away before it went any farther was quickly dismissed. She clasped his shirt in her fist, pulling him to her. She wanted it to go farther—much, much farther.

How odd. Such strange sensations surged through her mind and body. Never before had she been with a man, or even wanted to be. Her disastrous elopement at age fourteen had put a stop to all that. But now, with this electrifying man she just met, warmth radiated through her in a strange, new way. She stood cocooned inside his embrace, warm, and ready to explode. This is what it must feel like at the core of the earth—a magnetic pull so strong, nothing could stop it. Did everyone feel sparks when they met 'the one'?

At last he lowered his lips to hers—his moist, full lips. His romantic kiss was tender, yet powerful. When he deepened their kiss and pressed her into the wall, a strange and new passion engulfed her. Her mind swirled as Joe kissed her like she was the substance he needed to live. Or was it the other way around? She didn't know.

Knees sinking, Izetta dropped both arms to the wall at her back. Fanning her fingers out, they frantically searched for something. At the touch of his tongue, her hands stilled and she clawed her long nails into the floral wallpaper.

Joe buried both hands into her hair and caressed the back of her head, his thumbs massaging her temples.

She couldn't think to stop him. Instead she managed to lift one hand from the wall and slide it up his forearm. At last she got to caress one of the huge biceps teasing her all evening. The nerve endings in her fingertips came alive as she skimmed along his skin. Evidence of his years working on oilrigs showed in his rock hard muscles.

Suddenly her hand was empty. In a flash, he was out of her arms.

Izetta opened her eyes and found him a few feet away, gaping at her. His chest heaved as he sucked in air. Lips tingling, she searched his face before realizing his left hand gripped her front doorknob.

"I can't do this, Izetta."

Even in the dark, she could see the intensity in his eyes.

"You're an amazing woman. Funny, beautiful, intelligent. I want you for myself, but you're not mine to have. I'm sorry I kissed you." He yanked open the door.

"Don't be sorry." She pushed up from the wall. "I'm not sorry. I don't love Ford. I'm not sure why I ever accepted his proposal. I'll be breaking it off tomorrow."

Joe closed the gap between them in a single step. One hand shot to the back of her head and pulled her to his mouth. He kissed her with all the passion of moments ago, but this time he did not linger. His abrupt release caused her to wobble. Joe grabbed her waist and steadied her, before lowering for a final kiss.

Soft and tender, his kiss filled her with hope. Hope of what life could be like…what love could be like…what passion could be like.

"I'll call you when you're a free woman." The door snapped shut behind him, and Joe disappeared into the night's darkness.

CHAPTER NINE

As his face began to fade, panic rushed through her. "Don't leave. Come back, Joe," She pleaded as her hands clenched the steering wheel, squeezing it tight. "I need you." Had his spirit really been in the front seat with her, replaying memories in her mind's eye? Whatever it was, she never wanted it to stop.

Izetta sped past Blackwell's Corner and glanced down at her speedometer—almost ninety. On instinct, her foot let up on the gas. James Dean had crashed at that very spot on highway 466. She mustn't speed too.

The oversized steering wheel grew heavy in her grip and she adjusted her hands. All strength had evaporated from her body. Weeping took little physical movement, yet it drained all energy. When would the strength in her limbs return? She longed for the comfort of her bed where privacy and freedom allowed for hours reliving every minute of her time with the most amazing man she'd ever known. The only drawback to the seclusion were the nightmares. Relentless, terrifying nightmares. Not once had she made it through to morning without screaming herself awake. Ford haunted her sleep and Joe died in front of her night after night.

During the day, her nose betrayed her—the smell of gun powder clung to the inside of her nostrils. Blasts from the gun still reverberated in her ears. The endless barrage of memories drained the life right out of her. How could anyone survive the loss of a spouse?

She leaned forward and turned on the radio, pressing each

button for something comforting to listen to. At the sound of Perry Como's voice she stopped. As soon as she recognized the words to *Hello, Young Lovers*, she switched the radio off.

A headache pounded at the base of her skull. "Don't leave me, Joe." Dizziness swirled through her mind. Izetta teetered on a dangerous edge. Did she have any power to help herself?

A flash of Joe's lifeless face appeared, his eyes fixed and open, a trickle of blood escaping his lips. Nausea snaked through Izetta, and her foot clamped down on the accelerator as she climbed across the San Luis Obispo Mountain Range.

"Why, Joe? Why did you leave me?" Tears blurred her vision. She cursed Ford. "I wish I never met you." An instant stab sliced through her heart, for if she'd never met Ford, then she would never have met Joe. A debate sprouted in her mind as she zipped around the winding, mountainous curves. Would she rather have gone through life without experiencing amazing, all consuming love? Without meeting the one person who could steal her breath away and fill her heart at the same time? Yet, if she never met Ford, then Joe would still be alive.

Oh, why hadn't she gone out with Handsome Max? Her sisters tried to set her up with their younger brother-in-law. She should've listened.

Painful tremors raked through her body as she flew over the desert mountain range. A sheer cliff loomed eight hundred feet to the desert floor on one side of the rural highway. It alternated between an empty expanse and a rock wall where the road had been carved through the mountains.

Izetta wiped her eyes, blinking several times to clear her vision. She inspected the black sky out the big windshield. A layer of clouds muted the sliver of moon, and concealed the stars. She shouted through the cover. "Why God? Why did you let this happen?" Izetta smacked the steering wheel with the heel of her palm. "Why didn't you stop Ford?"

Since the night of the murder and suicide, she'd been wrestling with God. Never before had she felt such bone-wrenching betrayal. "You're supposed to be merciful and good. How is this good?" Her anger at the Lord kept gaining momentum since the funeral. All the

46

blame and fury she felt toward Ford often veered to the Lord. Why didn't He protect the only man she ever loved?

Cruel stabs sliced into her heart leaving it jagged and dismembered. How could anyone live in such agony? The grief was too intense—too torturous to bear.

The words of Job's wife in the Bible pierced her mind. "Curse God and die."

Izetta frowned.

Again the quote echoed inside. "Curse God and die."

Not a bad idea and easy enough with a cliff approaching on one side. *No.* She forced the wrong thought away. No matter how tempting, she could never do what Ford did and kill, not even herself. She'd wish that pain on no one, especially not her sweet Momma. Izetta's Christian upbringing and Momma's Bible quotes were rooted deep into her core. Though angry, she could never blaspheme the Lord.

The car's tires left the pavement and slid in gravel, spewing rocks and dust. Ice-water surged into her veins as she jerked the wheel, searching for the centerline. The headlight beams sliced through the darkness, reflecting the yellow line as she straightened her car.

I should have let it go over. Then I could be with Joe. As fast as it had entered, Izetta rejected the suicidal ideation. But ever so subtly, it crept back into the membranes of her mind, taunting her, as if begging to engage in conversation.

"I need you, Joe. I can't get through this without you!" No image of her beloved appeared in her mind's eye. "Come back to me. I don't want to be here without you."

Curse God and die. The evil voice hissed louder.

Again and again she tried to picture Joe's face, but could only draw a blank. An eerie foreboding swirled around her.

Just curse God and die. Put an end to your pain.

Izetta pointed the wheel at the black abyss ahead, pressed down on the gas pedal, and locked her elbows. She must get rid of the voices in her head. An image appeared of her sweet Momma on her knees and praying at her bedside, her face contorted as if in agony. Momma held Izetta's picture in one hand and her Bible in the other. Weeping, Momma whispered Izetta's name and the name of Jesus over and over.

The face of Jesus flickered before Izetta's eyes. One strong hand floated forward, light glowed through a dime sized hole at the base of His wrist. Jesus rested His hand on Izetta's shoulder. Heat flowed into her body. As she searched Christ's eyes, compassion and tenderness radiated from Him. It flooded her with peace and strength. She didn't have to bear the pain alone—Christ would help her if she'd just turn to Him.

It seemed to happen in slow motion, when in reality only a quick second had passed. Izetta slammed her brakes just as her wheels hit the loose gravel. She jerked the steering wheel hard, too hard. Tires spinning on their own agenda, careening her toward the cliff's edge, she buried the brake into the floorboard. The car fishtailed across the blacktop. Rocks jutting out on the other side of the road drew closer. She tried to point the car at the center lane, but the magnificent beast no longer obeyed her. It spun out of control, and smashed into a boulder the size of a dump truck.

Izetta's head jerked sideways and her skull went through the glass of her side window. Her entire bottom rose off the seat. When she came back through the hole, jagged pieces of glass tore the flesh on her neck, cheek, and jaw. Shattered fragments flew around her. The steering wheel crushed her chest. Somehow she bounced over to the passenger seat. Crumpled and beaten, the car finally screeched to a stop.

Izetta inhaled a slow, deep breath. *How odd.* She just wrecked her precious gift from Joe, but neither pain, or fear, or even sorrow plagued her. Only numbness—a complete void of sensation. *How truly odd.*

A trickle of warmth oozed from her nose and onto her lips. She could taste blood, but couldn't muster the strength to raise her hand and wipe it away. She gazed down and spotted blood on her lap. It looked like the ketchup on Joe's shirt when he played his awful joke.

Suddenly, Joe's face appeared in her mind's eye. He smiled. Soon his grin faded and morphed into the frozen, fixed look of that awful night. Blood dripped from his mouth. Instead of crying, Izetta cocked her head to the side and watched the slow trail of red dripping down her arm.

48

CHAPTER TEN

"Sarah."

Her eyes shot open. Sarah Triplett sat up and scanned her darkened bedroom. Who had called her name? She lived alone. Uneasiness snaked into her belly.

Sarah. The voice sounded again. It wasn't human. Although the hair on her arms perked up sending tingles across her skin, all fear disappeared. "Yes, God?" Never before had she heard the Lord so clear and piercing. Did the Holy Spirit wake her up by calling her name like so long ago with Samuel?

Pray.

When the gentle whisper once again filled Sarah's mind, a flash of her youngest daughter's face appeared in her mind. Sarah's breath caught. What was happening to Izetta? "Oh, Father, please help her."

Sarah jerked the quilt back, and slid to the floor. The clock on the nightstand read one o'clock. As she closed her eyes, her heart grew heavy. Something was very, very wrong. Perhaps she should get up and telephone Izetta's apartment at the beach. Or at least call over to Otha or Oma Belle. Maybe they knew what was happening.

PRAY! Fervor filled the word.

A sense of urgency overwhelmed Sarah. Knees cemented to the floor, she prayed aloud, opening her heart to the Lord. "Father God, please protect my daughter. Surround her with your angels. Forgive her anger with You over Joe's death—it's just the grief talking. She doesn't mean it—her pain is ghastly. You saved her from Ford's gun.

49

With all of my heart, I thank You. Now I ask for You to save her from whatever danger is threatening her tonight. She needs Your soothing love. Only You can rescue her from the pit of despair sucking her down. Save her, I pray in Jesus' name."

As the words flowed, the burden grew heavier. She folded her hands, squeezed her eyes shut, and lifted her voice to Heaven. "She was raised in Your house. Izetta grew up reading the Bible and going to church. Remind her of Your goodness. Have mercy on my daughter. Forgive her foolish talk. Restore her to You. Fill her with peace, and a renewed acceptance of Your Son into her heart."

***

Izetta shivered as she lay huddled in the front seat. The taste of blood filled her mouth. She rooted around with her tongue, but couldn't find any cuts. Where was the blood coming from? Shifting her focus to the scene in front of her face, the dashboard seemed far away, yet the steering wheel appeared close. Could she grab ahold and pull herself up? Perhaps she could drive to a hospital and they could stop the bleeding.

She reached forward. Pain pulsed through her body. She convulsed and dropped her hand. Izetta opened her mouth to scream but her chest refused to expand. Something pinned her down. When she mustered the strength to reach up again, the car began to spin as if she were drunk, and she fell into a black abyss.

***

Tears stung Sarah's eyes. No relief filtered into her soul. She added scriptures to her petitions. "God, you promised that if we raise a child in the way he should go, he would not depart from it when he is old. I have done my part. Please fulfil Your promise. You are a God of truth, honor, love, and mercy. You are not a man that You should lie."

The pit of her belly ached, doubling her over. All the way to the floor she sank and stretched out flat. The queasiness gained momentum. Should she get a bowl? Drenched in sweat, and on the verge of vomiting, Sarah whispered as many scriptures as she could remember. They seemed to pummel the inside of her mind, begging to be spoken aloud. As physical pain squeezed her heart, Sarah cried out to the Lord, praying His word aloud.

***

Izetta lifted her lids. *Keep yourself awake, honey.* Sleeping wouldn't be wise. Might it be smart to keep still until a car approached? She strained to distinguish any sounds. Nothing registered above the ringing in her ears—a loud relentless ring. She hummed a few seconds. When stopped, the ringing blared again.

A pool of blood filled her mouth and she swallowed. Its putrefied thickness oozed down her throat, gagging her. Soon, her mouth filled again. Izetta coughed, spewing blood everywhere. Inching toward the edge of the seat, she vomited onto the floorboard. *So much blood.* Where was it all coming from?

As the minutes passed, all strength drained from her body. Coldness crept into Izetta's feet. It coiled its way up her body. She convulsed again and her eyes lost focus, but her mind stayed clear. *I need help. I need it soon.*

***

Never before had such a ferocious burden wreak havoc through Sarah. The Holy Spirit had woken her to pray for Izetta—that message as clear as the grains of wood in her floor. Urgings from the Lord had stirred her before, but never anything like this. Fear threatened to overtake her, but Sarah shoved it away and filled her prayer with faith. "Father God, You did not kill Joe, but in Your infinite wisdom, You allowed it to happen. I don't know why, but I trust You. Joe was a good, Christian man. He is rejoicing in Heaven with You now. Show that to Izetta. Prod her to make peace with You before one day leaving this earth."

Yes.

Even though the Holy Spirit spoke another word to Sarah, it did

51

nothing to erase the burden. She sat up, tossed her head back and lifted her arms toward Heaven. "Restore Izetta to You. Save her from whatever calamity is threatening to overtake her."

***

Izetta struggled to roll her head to the side so she could see out the windshield. She searched for shadows dancing on boulders from approaching headlights. Only blackness surrounded her.

On a deserted highway in the dead of night, Izetta began to grasp the depth of her emergency. She needed a hospital soon. Very soon. Her gaze darted around the interior of the car, searching for something. She didn't know what. Back outside, she stared at the boulders. Still no lights or shadows appeared anywhere. No sounds. Only ringing. And blood. Lots of gagging blood.

A thought crept into her mind. This was all her fault. For a mere second she gave into Satan's temptation.

"I'm sorry." Her heart thundered in her chest, as if laboring to keep tempo with her thoughts. It took all her strength to keep her eyes open, for pain now surged through every muscle. Unable to endure it any longer, Izetta closed her eyes and gave into the syncope taking over.

***

Sarah jumped up as if her skin might erupt into flames. Unable to contain the boiling within, she paced and shouted more Bible verses. "Salvation belongs to God alone. Righteousness shall be upon my children. Believe on the Lord Jesus Christ and you shall be saved, you and your household. Christ is the only begotten Son."

An hour passed as she walked the floors. She entered her bedroom once more, and strode to her bureau. Sarah whisked up her Bible and dropped it onto the floor. It landed with a thud. Undaunted, she stepped atop the black leather, her bare toes hanging off the end. "I stand on Your promises, God. I believe everything You've said in this book. Your word does not return to You void. I trust You to

52

accomplish Your good purpose. Send Your angels to flight, I pray."

At last Sarah's voice lowered to a slow whisper and she collapsed onto the bed. Sobs begged to come out. Fear tempted her. She shoved both away. Nothing was too big for God. She trusted Him to fulfil every single promise He made.

***

When at last Izetta lifted her lids, it took a minute to wade through the fog. Why couldn't she sit up? Fuzziness blocked the memory and she began to panic, her breaths came in shallow puffs.

Joe's face appeared and Izetta relaxed. As usual he winked, but then his face morphed into a bouquet of roses. Her mother stood at the kitchen sink arranging them. A flash of her pet pigmy goat, Camille, came and stood by Izetta in a field of clover near her childhood farm in Oklahoma. The buzz of bees filled her ears but she didn't run or scream. She stood still, and just as daddy promised, none of them landed on her. Izetta watched daddy dig a deep grave for their dog. Specs of dirt stuck to the sweat dripping off his neck and forehead. A gunny sack lay at her feet. Duchess stuffed inside…dead from old age. Izetta's eyes filled with tears. Then Joe's face leaned over and kissed her cheek.

Each limb tingled, all strength had drained. More blood flooded her mouth. She couldn't bear to swallow it again and had no strength to spit it out. Tipping her face over the edge of the seat, she parted her lips and let the blood drip out.

Am I dying? It sounded absurd too far-fetched to be possible. She refused to entertain the surreal thought. Yet her chest tightened even more. She struggled to gulp in air. Wetness seemed to cover every body part. Was it blood or sweat?

***

Sarah glanced at the clock. Three A.M., she'd been at it for two hours, yet it seemed as quick as ten minutes. Once again she sunk to kneel on the floor. She opened her Bible to the page housing several

53

pictures. The one of Izetta taken last summer at Pismo Beach caught Sarah's eye. She kissed the image. Photo in one hand, the other clutching her Bible to her chest as if it were a life ring, Sarah thanked God for His perfection. She sang her favorite hymn written way back in time of Abraham Lincoln by the blind hymnist, Fanny Crosby. "Blessed assurance, Jesus is mine…"

As she sang, a peace seeped into her pores. It flooded her whole body and soul. Sarah took a deep inhale. Strength drained, she struggled to pull herself up. Is this what Michael the Arc Angel felt like after wrestling with the Prince of Persia for twenty-one days? Never before had Sarah engaged the enemy in such a way.

***

Izetta blinked as if to clear the cobwebs out of her mind. It worked and everything flooded back. Everything. *Curse God and die.* The evil hiss whispered to her once more. Izetta dug deep to fill her voice with firmness. "No. I rebuke you, Satan."

She focused on the Lord. "I'm sorry, Jesus." Her whisper barely audible even to herself, but she continued to speak aloud. "I'm sorry for blaming You. I'm sorry for my hateful thoughts."

For the first time, Izetta faced everything she had done. She had walked away from God several years ago. Not for any particular reason, she just stopped going to church. Business, laziness, and earthly desires captured her time. She'd never been on fire or sold out the way people talk about, so it was easy to sleep in on Sunday after a night of drinking at the dance hall. She never bothered to pray for her food anymore, or before closing her eyes at night. Next thing she knew, she rarely thought of the Lord. Until Joe. And then he was murdered. She never said aloud that she hated God, but the words begged to come out. Her thoughts had become horrific. "Please forgive me, Lord."

Izetta licked her lips. Despite the blood, they seemed parched and ready to split. If only she hadn't ignored Ford's threats. She didn't understand what he meant about giving them two weeks. It never occurred to her that Ford planned to end Joe's life. Why hadn't she talked to him about it? Maybe he could have stopped Ford, after all, they used to be close friends. She thought she'd been protecting Joe from the law if he had lost his temper. Her husband was bigger and stronger than Ford. Yet if she had trusted him, maybe he could have thwarted Ford's plans. At a minimum, Izetta should have prayed and asked God for help, like she used to do as a young girl. What happened to her childhood faith?

"Oh, Jesus, I've been blaming You instead of Ford—been angry with You instead of me for ignoring the warnings. I'm sorry." The pounding of her heart intensified as she made up with her Savior. Izetta asked Jesus to take her back, like they had broken up. Not that He had left her, but she had left Him. "Please forgive me."

***

A tiny light on the far side of the room caught Sarah's eye. It grew bright as it closed in on her. The light shone on a church. Its doors opened wide and the inside of the sanctuary came into view. Sunrays filtered through the stained-glass windows. Clear and beautiful, the vision seemed real, like she could reach out and touch it. Sarah didn't move as she soaked in the miraculous vision before her.

The bright scene narrowed to the front church pew. There, Izetta had stretched out, eyes closed and feet crossed at the ankles. She wore the lavender paisley dress Sarah had sewn for her last Easter. Izetta's golden hair shimmered under a beam from the strained-glass window. She clutched a large, gold cross in her hands. A sweet smile lifted the corners of Izetta's lips. Her whole countenance exuded peace and seemed to glow. Never before had Sarah seen such tranquility on her daughter's flawless skin. Ethereal. Divine. At peace.

Seconds later, the vision muted and floated up through the ceiling like a fluffy white cloud moving in the sky.

"Don't go." Sarah stared until the last speck of light disappeared, memorizing every detail. What did it mean? Why did the Lord give the vision to her?

A swift answer penetrated her heart—God had answered her prayers. Izetta would make peace with Him and belong to Christ for

55

eternity.

Comfort filled Sarah. If not tonight, someday very soon, her daughter would let go of all the bitterness she harbored toward the Lord. Sarah didn't know when, but took solace in the assurance that it would happen before Izetta moved off this earth. "Thank you, Lord."

Gone was the putrid acid filling Sarah earlier. A warm fragrance, like baked cinnamon apples, filled the air and soothed her. At last she slipped under the covers and breathed in peace. Her youngest child would be just fine.

***

A lightness washed over Izetta, along with a perplexing calmness. "I feel myself drifting away from this world. I trust You, Jesus. Receive me into Your presence. Please take care of my momma, though. Don't let this hurt her real bad. Cradle her in Your arms, and receive me into Your arms, in Jesus' name. Amen."

Izetta's mind stopped spinning, as if the car whipping around and around had finally stilled. All coldness faded away. Weightlessness filtered in. Her body light and airy. No panic, no fear, just sweet love cradling her.

When blackness sought to overtake her, Izetta didn't fight it. A pin hole of light shone ahead and she focused on its approach. *Thank You, Jesus. I see You.* Izetta closed her eyes and whispered, "I'm coming, Joe."

~ The End ~

Author's Note:

My Great Granny, Sarah Triplett, often talked about the amazing vision she experienced the night Izetta died. God woke her up to pray. Sarah did so for two hours. She then received the vision of Izetta lying on a church pew. Great Granny knew the vision meant Izetta would make her peace with God. She'd dwell with Him some day. Granny had no idea it would happen that very night, May 8th, 1960.

In the early morning hours of Mother's Day, the police knocked on Sarah's door. They delivered the horrific news of Izetta's death. The autopsy showed the cause as internal bleeding. The Medical Examiner said it took about two hours for Izetta to bleed to death. The time coincided with Sarah being woken to pray, and then receiving the vision.

According to the police, skid marks showed how Izetta had braked and swerved away from the cliff's edge. Whether she fell asleep, or had been speeding and lost control, we do not know. It even could have been from blurred vision due to crying. Regardless, the police ruled it as an accident, and not intentional due to the braking skid marks. We only know God gave Granny the vision to assure her of Izetta's acceptance into Heaven. This gave great peace to Granny Sarah—a peace that lasted the rest of her life.

Most of the details written in this story are true, although Joe and Ford's names were changed. Izetta's name and her family member's names were not changed. Those are real, as well as Izetta's elopement at age fourteen. She stormed home that night and wouldn't tell anyone what happened. We can only guess.

One of the liberties taken was adding six years to Izetta's date of birth. The only reason I did this was to weave in details of Great Granny sewing parachutes during WWII. She supervised the seamstresses who sewed and packed parachutes. The family was very proud of her contributions to the war effort. This liberty was simply to honor her.

Also true was Izetta's second elopement many years later. She married her fiancé's best friend. The ex-fiancé told everyone he'd give the newlyweds two weeks only. No one knew what he meant. In those days, no one thought the worst. So on the night of Izetta's fourteenth wedded day, 'Ford' snuck into her house and killed 'Joe.' Ford told a naked Izetta, huddling on the floor, how he meant to shoot her as well, but couldn't make himself pull the trigger. He then drank a beer from her fridge and shot himself in the head. At the time of the murder/suicide, 'Ford' was forty years old, had never been married, and was a wealthy millionaire.

When Izetta's body arrived at the funeral home from the morgue, her rare star sapphire wedding ring was missing. Izetta loved that ring. She never would have taken it off. Police, ambulance, medical examiner, and mortician all denied seeing it at the scene or when Izetta's body arrived at their facilities. Its whereabouts are still a mystery. Perhaps it's hidden in the crack of a boulder somewhere in the San Luis Obispo Mountains.

Another mystery is why Izetta ever accepted Ford's proposal in the first place. No one in the family understood that. Joe, on the other hand, everyone understood. No two people appeared more in love than Joe and Izetta. They were crazy about each other. I look forward to meeting them both in Heaven.

***

Sarah Triplett, born September 13th, 1900, lived 90 years and died on 1/24/1991. She really did have hair to her knees that she braded, and then wrapped in a ring around her head.

Not a Marilyn Monroe lookalike in the face, Izetta Conkey was pretty nonetheless. She had adorable dimples and lovely eyes. She was known as a classy lady who never uttered a curse word.

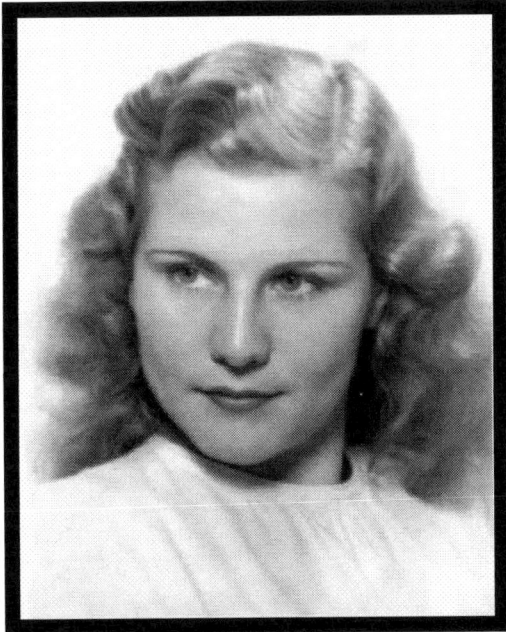

IZETTA CONKEY
IN LOVING MEMORY
1923   1960

Made in the USA
Columbia, SC
01 January 2019